Fishing

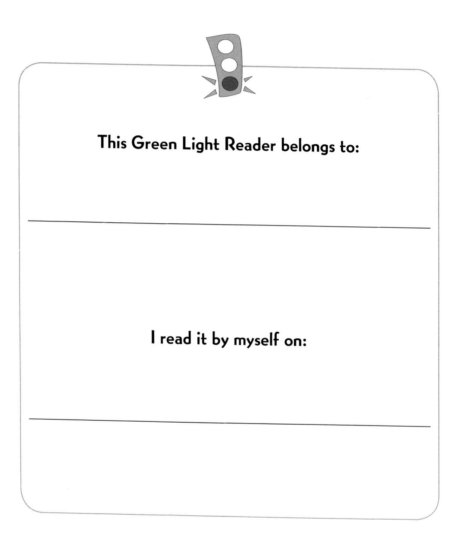

This Green Light Reader belongs to:

_____

I read it by myself on:

_____

Fishing

A Mr. and Mrs. Green
Adventure

KEITH BAKER

sandpiper

HOUGHTON MIFFLIN HARCOURT
Boston   New York

The text of this book was set in Giovanni Book.
The illustrations were done in acrylic paint on illustration board.

For Laurie,

with great, green gratitude

Mr. Green reeled in a fish.
"Another one!" he said.
"That makes 14.
 I *love* fishing!"

Mrs. Green loved fishing, too—
only not today.

Today her pail was empty.

But Mrs. Green was full
of determination.

"Let's switch places," she said.
"All the fish are on *your*
side of the boat."

"Gladly," said Mr. Green.
(He liked fishing from either side.)

So they switched places.

The boat wobbled back and forth

(Mr. Green almost fell in.)

They cast their lines out into the water.
Mrs. Green felt ready and steady—
she would catch the next fish.

But she didn't.

"Number 15," said Mr. Green.

"The biggest one yet!"

Mrs. Green had another idea.

"Let's trade fishing poles,"
she said.
"Your pole is shiny
and new."

"With pleasure," said Mr. Green.
(He liked fishing with any pole.)

Mrs. Green felt ready
and steady and sure.

13

But not for long.

"Fan-fish-tas-tic!" said Mr. Green.

"Number 16!

8 + 8 . . . 4 x 4 . . . $\frac{1}{2}$ of 32—

that's 16."

8 + 8   16   4 + 4

½ of 32

"Oh, I do love fishing!" he said.

Mrs. Green was not
sharing his enthusiasm.
She felt frustrated
and fishless.

She had one more idea.

"May I wear your hat?
It must be lucky."

"Lucky?" asked Mr. Green.

"No, my lucky hat is at home."

"Then *how*," asked Mrs. Green,

"are you catching all those fish?"

"Jelly beans!" said Mr. Green.

"Gooey, chewy, yummy, gummy
jelly beans.
These fish love 'em."

"I have a jelly bean system.
Cinnamon on stormy days,
green apple on misty days,
bubble gum on cloudy days,
watermelon on windy days,
root beer on foggy days,
and peppermint on sunny days—
like today!"

"And these licorice ones are good *any* time."

"Jelly bean?" asked Mr. Green.

"Peppermint, please," said Mrs. Green.

She slipped the jelly bean onto her hook.
She cast her line far out into the water.
She prepared herself for the catch, but . . .

. . . no nibbles . . .

. . . no bites . . .

. . . no fish.

Mr. Green was perplexed.
His system wasn't working.
Had the jelly bean slipped off?
Was it the wrong flavor?
Were the fish full?

Then all of a sudden, Mrs. Green felt
a tug and a jiggle,
then a wiggle and a yank.

"Jumping jelly beans," she shouted,
"I CAUGHT ONE!"

"Number 17!" said Mr. Green.

"And it's a beauty."

"Oh, I do love fishing," said Mrs. Green.

"I wonder . . .

. . . what we could catch with
chocolate chip cookies."

About the Author

Keith Baker has written and illustrated many well-loved picture books and early chapter books, including several about the charming and lovable Mr. and Mrs. Green. He lives in Seattle, Washington. Visit his website at www.KeithBakerBooks.com.

Picture Books by Keith Baker

Big Fat Hen

Potato Joe

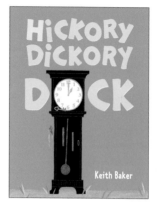

Hickory Dickory Dock

Hide and Snake

Who Is the Beast?

The Magic Fan

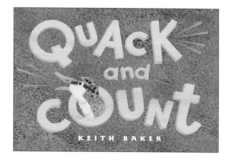

Quack and Count

Camping: A Mr. and Mrs. Green Adventure
Keith Baker

Cookies: A Mr. and Mrs. Green Adventure
Keith Baker

Fishing: A Mr. and Mrs. Green Adventure
Keith Baker

The Talent Show: A Mr. and Mrs. Green Adventure
Keith Baker

George and Martha
James Marshall

George and Martha: Two Great Friends
James Marshall

George and Martha: Round and Round
James Marshall

George and Martha: Rise and Shine
James Marshall

George and Martha: One More Time
James Marshall

Martha Speaks: Haunted House
Susan Meddaugh

Martha Speaks: Play Ball
Susan Meddaugh

Martha Speaks: Toy Trouble
Susan Meddaugh

My Robot
Eve Bunting/Dagmar Fehlau

Soccer Song
Patricia Reilly Giff/Blanche Sims

**Catch Me If You Can!/
¡A que no me alcanzas!**
Bernard Most

A Butterfly Grows
Steven R. Swinburne

**Daniel's Mystery Egg/
El misterioso huevo de Daniel**
Alma Flor Ada/G. Brian Karas

Moving Day
Anthony G. Brandon/Wong Herbert Yee

**Digger Pig and the Turnip/
Marranita Poco Rabo y el nabo**
Caron Lee Cohen/Christopher Denise

**The Chick That Wouldn't Hatch/
El pollito que no quería salir del huevo**
Claire Daniel/Lisa Campbell Ernst

Get That Pest!/¡Agarren a ése!
Erin Douglas/Wong Herbert Yee

Snow Surprise
Lisa Campbell Ernst

On the Way to the Pond
Angela Shelf Madearis/Lorinda Bryan Caul

Little Red Hen Gets Help
Kenneth Spengler/Margaret Spengler

Tumbleweed Stew/Sopa de matojos
Susan Stevens Crummel/Janet Stevens
Alma Flor Ada/F. Isabel Campoy

Coming Soon to Green Light Readers!

ris and Walter
lissa Haden Guest

ris and Walter: The Sleepover
lissa Haden Guest

ris and Walter and Baby Rose
lissa Haden Guest

ris and Walter and Cousin Howie
lissa Haden Guest

. Brand-New Day with Mouse and Mole
Vong Herbert Yee

Aouse and Mole: A Perfect Halloween
Vong Herbert Yee

)odsworth in Rome
im Egan

Mouse and Mole: Fine Feathered Friends
Wong Herbert Yee

Mouse and Mole: A Winter Wonderland
Wong Herbert Yee

Upstairs Mouse, Downstairs Mole
Wong Herbert Yee

Abracadabra! Magic with Mouse and Mole
Wong Herbert Yee

Dodsworth in London
Tim Egan

Dodsworth in New York
Tim Egan

Dodsworth in Paris
Tim Egan